The Sweetest One of All

By
Jean Little

Illustrated by
Marisol Sarrazin

North Winds Press
An imprint of Scholastic Canada Ltd.

The illustrations in this book were created in chalk pastels on special pastel paper.

The text type was set in 20 point Minister Book.

Library and Archives Canada Cataloguing in Publication
Little, Jean, 1932-
The sweetest one of all / Jean Little ; Marisol Sarrazin, illustrator.
ISBN 978-0-439-93775-7
I. Sarrazin, Marisol, 1965- II. Title.
PS8523.I77S93 2008   jC813'.54   C2008-900849-9

ISBN-10 0-439-93775-2

6 5 4 3 2 1   Printed in Singapore   08 09 10 11 12 13

For Eleanor LeFave, who started me off; for Jenny Stephens, who kept me
going; and for the Felker girls — Elsie, Annabelle, Jane and Heather —
with my love.
— J.L.

To Marc, my love, with whom I hope to have the sweetest one of all.
— M.S.

The lamb looked up at the sheep.

"Who are you?" she asked.

"I am your mother," the ewe told her.

"Who am I?" the lamb asked then.

"You," the sheep said, "are the loveliest lamb in the land."

The cow looked down at the skipping lamb.

"I wish I had a lamb," she said.

"Nonsense," said the sheep, with a laugh.

"You don't want a lamb. You want a calf."

"You're right!" said the cow.

The calf gazed up at the cow.

"Who are you?" she asked.

"I am your mother," the cow said gently.

"Then who am I?" asked the calf.

"You," said the cow, "are the cutest calf in the clover."

The mare watched the nuzzling calf.
"I want a little calf like that," she said.
"That's silly," said the cow.
"What you really want is a filly."
"Of course," said the horse.

"Who are you?" the foal asked the horse.

"I am your mother," the mare said.

"And who am I?" the foal asked.

"You," said the horse, "are the finest foal in the field."

The pig looked at the wobbly foal.
"I wish I had a filly," she said.

"Don't be silly," said the horse. "You want piglets."

"Good plan," said the pig.

"Horse sense," said the mare.

The smallest piglet snuggled up to the big mother pig.

"Who are you?" she asked.

"I am your mother," said the sow.

"Who am I, then?" squeaked the piglet.

"You," said the pig, "are the perkiest piglet in the pen."

The nanny goat watched the wriggling piglets.

"I want some piglets too," she said.

The billy goat snorted and shook his head.

"We're goats," he said. "You'll have a kid."

"Not me," said the nanny goat. "I'm having twins."

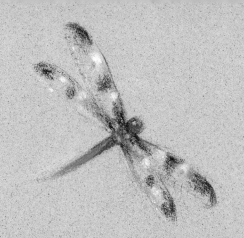

"Who are you?" the first kid asked.

"And who are we?" asked the second.

"She is your mother," said the billy goat.

"And you," said the nanny, "are the friskiest kids in the kingdom."

The goose watched the kids leaping and larking about.
"I want some baby goats," she said.
"Oh, you don't want a couple of kids,"
said the nanny. "You want a gaggle of goslings."
"Goodness gracious!" giggled the goose,
checking her eggs. "I think I've got some."

21

The goslings gazed up at the goose.

"Who are you?" they asked.

"I am your mother," the goose announced.

"Then who are we?" the goslings wanted to know.

"You," she told them, "are the most glorious goslings in the garden."

The dog gazed at the goslings.
"How dear they all are!" she said. "I want some too."
"No, no, no!" the goose said. "What you want is a pup."

The puppy opened her eyes.

"Am I a kitten?" she asked her mother.

"No, you are not," the dog said, kissing her button nose.

"You are the most perfect puppy on the planet."

"Look who's new," a mother said to her baby, pointing to the animals one by one.

"They all have beautiful babies," she said.
"But you are MY little one,
and you are the sweetest one of all."
"Mama," said the little one, hugging her. "Mama."